# LESSONS
### OF A LAC

This book will give your child a unique way to think about their worries. Having an understanding of their anxiety or 'worry feelings' gives them empowerment. Learning that there is an alternative to worrying all the time gives them some relief.

Loppy the LAC (**L**ittle **A**nxious **C**reature) and Curly Calmster will help your child realize that just because dangerous things *might* happen, doesn't mean they *will*.

Visit **www.lessonsofalac.com** to find out about more books in the series.

For the wonderful mix of Loppy LACs and Curly Calmsters in my life – L.J.

For my mum, who taught me to draw and taught me to love – K.L.

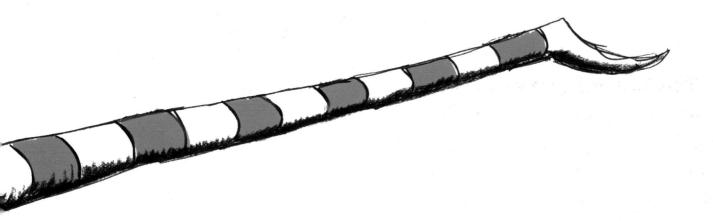

# LESSONS OF A LAC

Lynn Jenkins

*illustrated by*

Kirrili Lonergan

EK

This is the story of a LAC named Loppy.
LACs live in a village on one
side of a big mountain.

LACs have big muscles in their eyes and lips.
So their eyes are really **googly**
and their lips really **huge!**

LACs go to school.
They are taught how to look out for danger.
Their extra special skill is 'scary talk' like:

'What if ...'

and 'I'm never going to be able to,'

and 'I don't think I can,'

and 'Oh, no!'

The LACs have an enemy:
the Calmsters.

Calmsters live on the other
side of the big mountain.

At their school, they are taught how
to create calm and peace. Their extra
special skill is 'soothing talk' like:

'It's okay,'

and 'I can do it,'

and 'Breathe'

and 'I might try it'.

The LACs and Calmsters have always battled. They take their battles very seriously because when one wins, the other Shrinks.

One day, Loppy climbed to the top of the big mountain.
*I need to spy on the enemy so they can't trick me,* he thought.
Loppy looked down at the Calmster village.

'Oh no! That's Curly Calmster looking back at me!'

Loppy's heart beat faster, his arms and legs went stiff and his breathing became rapid.

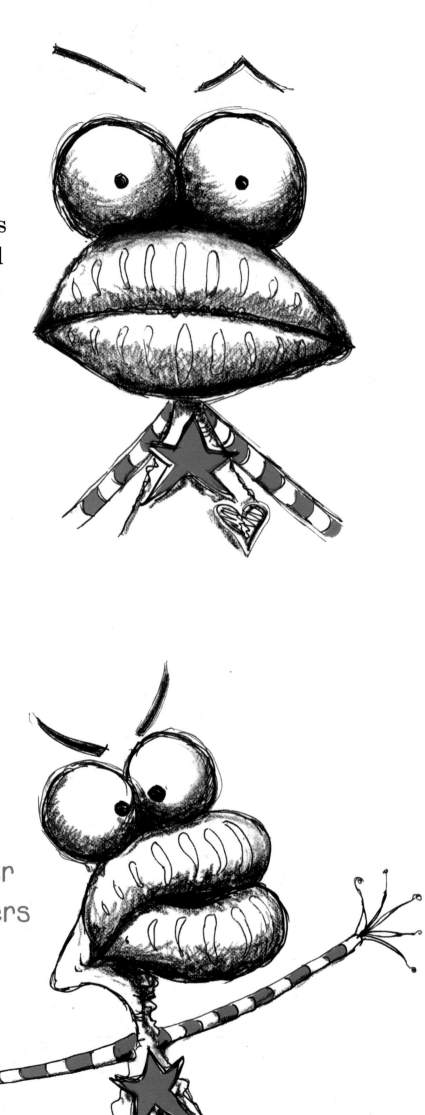

'What if Curly Calmster calls the other Calmsters to battle?'

'I'm so silly
for coming here!'

'What if the sun shines
off my binoculars and
other Calmsters see
me? Oh, no!'

Loppy's heart beat even faster,
his arms and legs went even stiffer,
and his breathing became even more
rapid with each thought.

Loppy looked back.

'Oh no! Curly's floating up toward me!'

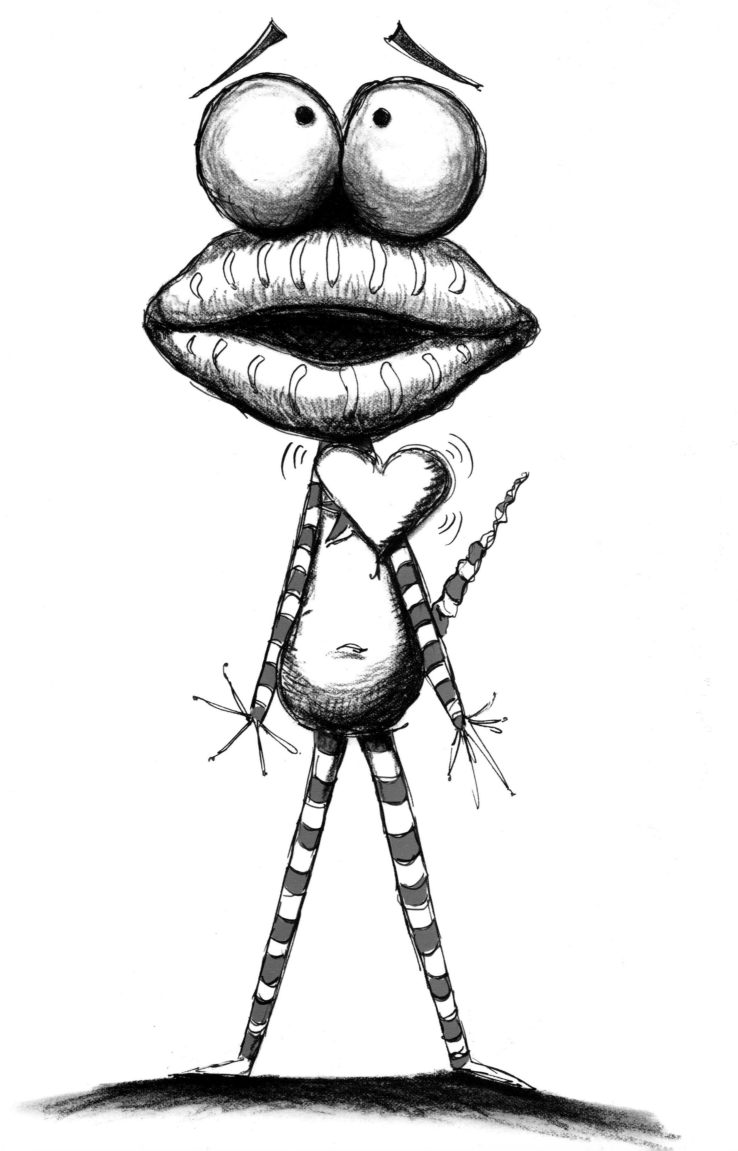

Loppy stood firm.
'You can't defeat me!'

'It's okay! You don't have
to battle me,' said Curly.

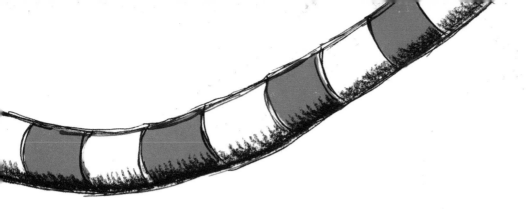

'Don't I?' Loppy felt confused.

'No,' replied Curly. 'I know you think you're doing your job when you look out for danger, but you don't *always* have to look for the danger in things.'

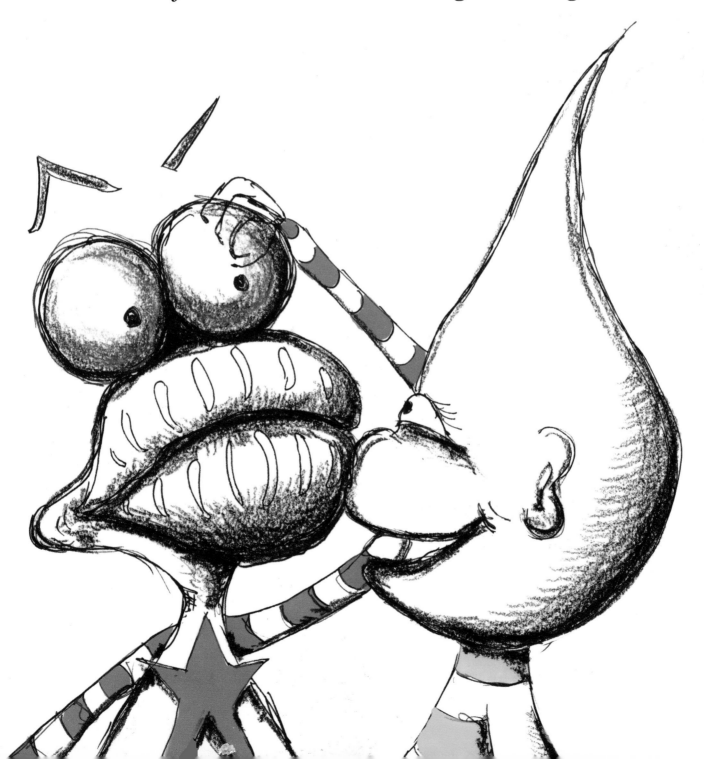

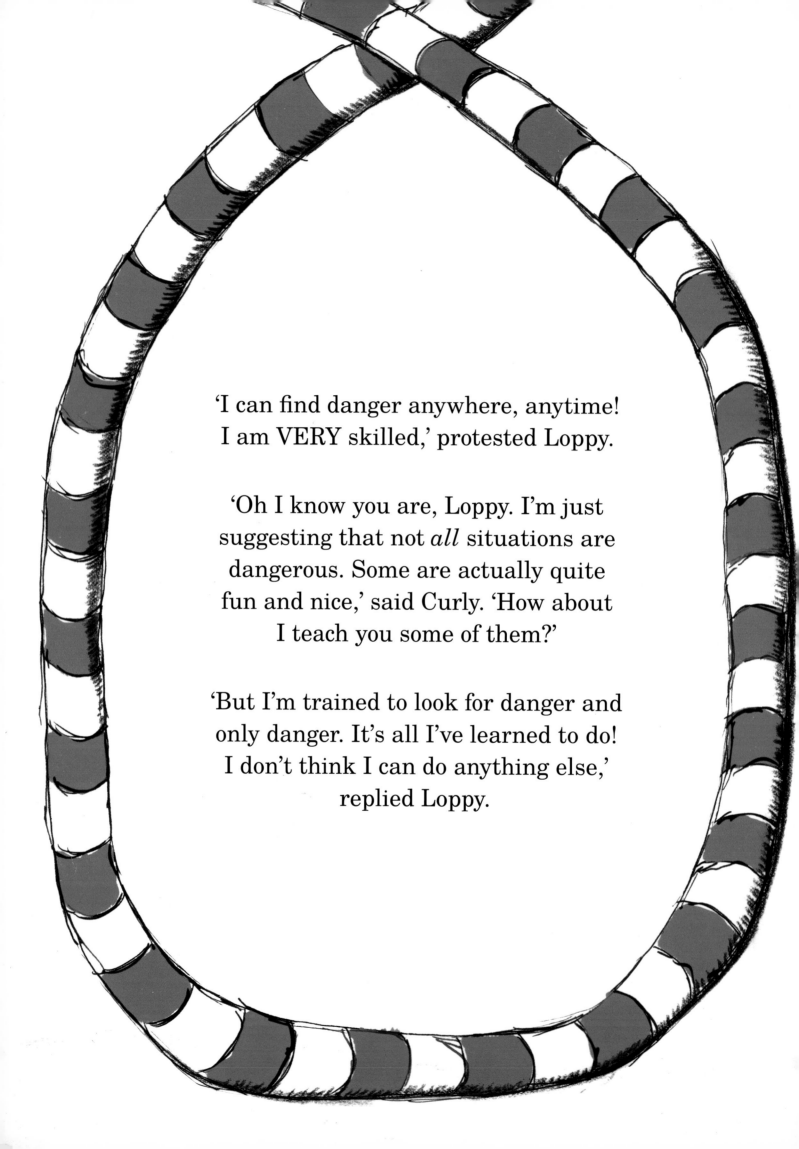

'I can find danger anywhere, anytime!
I am VERY skilled,' protested Loppy.

'Oh I know you are, Loppy. I'm just
suggesting that not *all* situations are
dangerous. Some are actually quite
fun and nice,' said Curly. 'How about
I teach you some of them?'

'But I'm trained to look for danger and
only danger. It's all I've learned to do!
I don't think I can do anything else,'
replied Loppy.

'Just fill your belly with a deep breath,' Curly said. 'Let it out and say, "I don't always have to look for danger. I don't always have to use scary talk. Just because dangerous things MIGHT happen doesn't mean they WILL happen." '

Loppy did as Curly said. Loppy had never taken slow deep breaths before. Loppy had never thought those sorts of thoughts before. For the first time, Loppy felt calm and peaceful.

'Maybe I can work with you. I won't always look for danger,' Loppy said.

They shook hands and went back to their villages to spread the word.

Soon there was a new village. It was on the very top of the big mountain. Both the LACs and the Calmsters lived there together. Loppy learned that danger *wasn't* always around.

And in fact, when he started to look for fun instead, Loppy saw that it was

# everywhere!

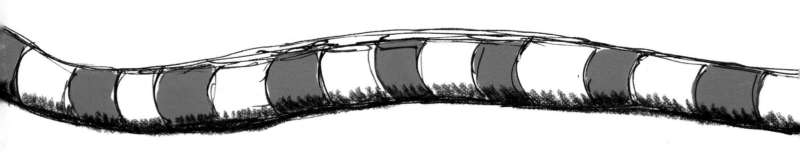

'Oh, it's a LAC's life for me!'
said Loppy smiling.

First published 2014 by Little Steps Publishing
This edition published 2018 by EK Books

EK Books
an imprint of Exisle Publishing Pty Ltd
PO Box 864, Chatswood, NSW 2057, Australia
226 High Street, Dunedin, 9016, New Zealand
www.ekbooks.org

A CiP record for this book is available from the National Library of Australia.

ISBN 978-1-925335-82-8

Original design adapted by Big Cat Design
Typeset in TeX Gyra  Schola 18 on 22pt
Printed in China

This book uses paper sourced under ISO 14001 guidelines from
well-managed forests and other controlled sources.

2 4 6 8 10 9 7 5 3 1